The Pumpkin Patch

For my mother, another McNamara
—M. M.

SIMON SPOTLIGHT
An imprint of Simon & Schuster Children's Publishing Division
1230 Avenue of the Americas, New York, NY 10020
This Simon Spotlight edition July 2021
First Aladdin Paperbacks edition September 2003
Text © 2003 by Simon & Schuster, Inc. Illustrations © 2003 by Mike Gordon
All rights reserved, including the right of reproduction in whole or in part in any form.
SIMON SPOTLIGHT, READY-TO-READ, and colophon are
registered trademarks of Simon & Schuster, Inc.
For information about special discounts for bulk purchases, please contact
Simon & Schuster Special Sales at 1-866-506-1949 or business@simonandschuster.com.
Manufactured in the United States of America 0621 LAK
2 4 6 8 10 9 7 5 3 1
Cataloging-in-Publication Data was previously supplied for the paperback edition of this title from
the Library of Congress.
Library of Congress Cataloging-in-Publication Data
McNamara, Margaret.
The pumpkin patch / Margaret McNamara ; illustrated by Mike Gordon.
p. cm. — (Robin Hill School) "Ready-to-read."
Summary: Katie finds what she thinks is the perfect pumpkin on a class field trip to a pumpkin
patch, but after her classmates tease her about how small it is, it is up to Katie's father to show
her how perfect her pumpkin can be.
[1. Pumpkins—Fiction. 2. Field trips—Fiction.] I. Gordon, Mike, ill. II. Title.
III. Series: McNamara, Margaret. Robin Hill School.
PZ7.M232518Pu 2003 [E]—dc21 2002155809
ISBN 978-1-5344-8535-8 (hc)
ISBN 978-0-689-85874-1 (pbk)

The Pumpkin Patch

Written by Margaret McNamara
Illustrated by Mike Gordon

Ready-to-Read

Simon Spotlight

New York   London   Toronto   Sydney   New Delhi

"Put on your coats!"
said Mrs. Connor.

Mrs. Connor's class
was going
on a field trip
to the pumpkin patch!

Katie was ready first.
She could not wait
to find
the perfect pumpkin.

The bus ride was long.

The whole time,
Katie imagined
the perfect pumpkin.

At the pumpkin patch
there were lots and lots
of pumpkins.

"You may each
take home
one pumpkin,"
said Mrs. Connor.
"Choose carefully."

Katie began
her search.

She looked
under vines.

She looked in
the straw.

She looked
in the mud.

At last Katie found it—
the perfect pumpkin!

Mrs. Connor's class
got back on the bus.

They showed off
their pumpkins.

"Mine is round,"
said Emma.

"Mine is tall,"
said Ayanna.

"Mine is big," said Neil.

"Look at Katie's pumpkin!"
said James.
"It is so small."

Katie's pumpkin was small.
It was very, very small.

Katie felt bad.
Her pumpkin
was not perfect.

Katie took her pumpkin home.

"I picked a bad pumpkin,"
she told her dad.

"That is not a bad pumpkin,"
he said.
"It is a good pumpkin.
Let me show you."

Katie's dad
cooked the pumpkin.
Then he cut it
into pieces.

Katie mashed the pieces.

And they made a pie.

Katie took the pie
to school.

"My pumpkin was small,"
she said.

"But it was sweet!
Now it is a pie."

The children loved
Katie's pumpkin pie.
"Your pumpkin was perfect!"
said James.